What Can Matt Do?

by Ellen Appelbaum
illustrated by Shelly Shinjo

Harcourt

Orlando   Boston   Dallas   Chicago   San Diego

Visit *The Learning Site!*
www.harcourtschool.com

Matt ran up and down.

Oh, look at Matt go!

What can Matt see?

Matt can tap.
Matt can tap it.

Can Matt go in?

Yes, Matt can go in.

Look! Here we come.